think
and
make
like
an artist

Thames & Hudson

Claudia Boldt and Eleanor Meredith

think and make like an artist © 2017
Claudia Boldt and Eleanor Meredith

Written and art-directed
by Claudia Boldt and Eleanor Meredith,
founders of The Loop

Edited
by Georgia Amson-Bradshaw

Designed
by Shaz Mandani

Original illustrations
by Jay Daniel Wright and Ola Niepsuj

Activities made
by Laura Bird

First published in the United States of
America in 2017 by Thames & Hudson Inc.,
500 Fifth Avenue, New York, New York 10110

www.thamesandhudsonusa.com

Reprinted 2018

Library of Congress Control Number
2016955403

ISBN 978-0-500-65098-1

Printed and bound in China by Reliance
Printing (Shen Zhen) Co., Ltd.

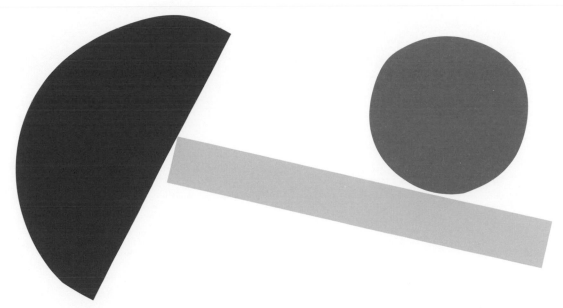

This book is about art.
First it makes you think about art, then you can
have fun making some art. Along the way,
look at the work of artists for plenty of good ideas.

CONTENTS

6

Imagine a work of art.
What do you see?
Is it a painting? A sculpture?
A photograph?
Think about that work of art.
Who made it?
How? And why?

Think

Where do artists get ideas from? Every artist will give you a different answer. They might find inspiration in a walk in the park, or watching people in a café. Sometimes artists think very big thoughts, about important ideas like freedom, fairness or the future. Other times their ideas are very personal, all about their feelings. Or they might simply be exploring, having fun.

Make

There are lots of different types of art, such as painting, photography, drawing, costume design, or sculpture. Artists choose to work in one way or another because it works well with the thought they want to share.

Art

So when an artist has an idea, a message, or a thought that they care about, they make something to share this thought. Put these two things together, the thinking and the making, and you get art.

In this book you will find activities exploring different ideas, and meet exciting artists making art in different ways. So let's think and make like an artist!

8

paint

Understanding the world through painting

What is a painting?

Playing with pictures

1

For thousands of years, artists painted people and objects to look like they did in real life.

What is it?

This is not art!

2

Then, in the early 20th century, artists stopped trying to make paintings look realistic. Instead, they painted wild pictures full of strange shapes and colors. Many people found this "new" art very shocking.

3

But abstract art was not really as new as people thought. Neanderthals painted abstract shapes on the walls of caves 40,000 years ago!

4

The 20th century was a time of great change. During the world wars, some abstract artists tried to escape the harsh reality of life through painting.

5

Abstract artists simplify the world in their pictures to help them understand it better.

6

Abstract art is full of bold colors and geometric shapes. Turn the page to see an abstract painting by artist Cornelia Baltes.

9

<u>Cornelia Baltes</u> has made this abstract painting. Its name is "Dingbats." Dingbats doesn't just hang around on walls like other paintings. It stands on two legs, like an actor on a stage.

Hello, Dingbats!

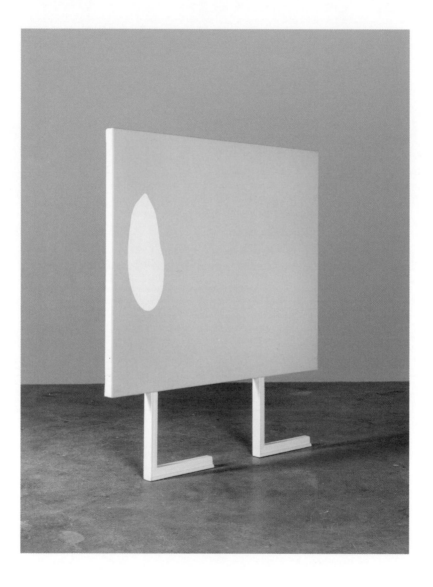

"I was resting the painting on wood.
It was suddenly obvious:
The work should have legs!"

Do you have a favorite painter?

Paint an angry squiggle, and a happy squiggle.

Play with paint

11

Paint things with personalities. Scary buttons, or hungry peas?

Mix a happy color. Mix a sad color.

Paint an ant using simple shapes.

Objects with attitude

My family and eye

Cornelia Baltes used legs to give her painting personality.
Make everyday objects come alive!

→ YOU WILL NEED:
A few objects from your kitchen. Sticky tape.
Scissors. Pencil. Card. Paints. Paintbrushes.

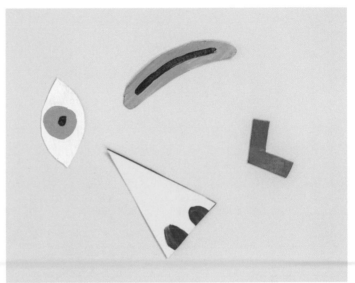

1. On a piece of card, draw body parts like arms, legs, noses and mouths in pencil.

2. Paint all the body parts on the card, then cut them out when the paint is dry.

13

3. Find some objects you want to bring alive. We are starting with a ketchup bottle.

4. Sticky tape the body parts to the objects, then put them back where you found them to give your family a surprise!

Painting with shapes

Abstract art inspired by nature

14

Which simple shapes make up a twig?
Create beautiful collages with painted paper.

→ YOU WILL NEED:
Several pieces of paper or card. Paints. Paintbrushes. Scissors. Glue.
Natural objects.

1. Begin by painting the pieces of paper in colors you like. Bright colors work well. Lay out the pieces to dry.

2. Collect plants and stones from a park, or use books and the internet to find pictures of things you like.

15

3. Look carefully at your collection. When the paper is dry, cut out the shapes and patterns you see.

4. Arrange the cut-outs onto a piece of painted paper. Look at the shapes but also consider the space between. Glue it in place.

16

sculpt

Sculptures can make us think,
change our opinions and even take action

Why make sculptures?

How artists try to change our opinions

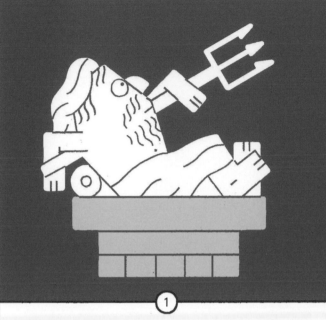

1

2

For centuries artists have been asked to impress the public with sculptures of their gods, kings, queens and leaders.

Who asks for sculptures to be made?
Good question. Sometimes a country might want to put across a message, such as "we won the war" or "let's celebrate peace."

3

4

Today, many artists create sculptures that show their own personal political opinions, rather than the opinions of their country or government.

The sculptures talk about important issues, like how we treat each other and the planet. On the next page you will find James Dive's witty protest sculpture about global warming.

James Dive is a sculptor who loves and hates
the hot Australian summers. His sculpture
of an ice cream truck melting is funny but it
also makes us think about global warming.

It's named after a weather forecast:
"Hot with a chance of a late storm."

18

"Imagine a place so hot that even
the ice cream truck melts."

Where can you show your sculpture?
Will many people see it?

What would you like your sculpture to talk about?

Love
or
hate

What do you want to change?

Can you think of big and small things that make you angry?

Ice sculptures

These ice sculptures melt and remind us of the current weather — is it unusually hot?

→ YOU WILL NEED:
Empty yoghurt pots. Interesting objects, such as leaves, shells,
or cut-up pieces of colored paper. String. Water. A freezer.

1. Find interesting objects, such as leaves, shells and cut-up pieces of colored paper. Clean some empty yoghurt pots.

2. Place your interesting objects inside the pots and fill them up with water.

3. Place a looped piece of string into the water, with one end of the loop hanging out. Place the pots in the freezer overnight.

4. Once completely frozen, pop the ice sculptures out of their yoghurt pots and hang them somewhere outside to watch them melt.

Underwater city

Our sea levels are rising because of global warming.
Make a sculpture that makes people think.

→ YOU WILL NEED:
Polymer clay in several colors. Rolling pin. Butter knife. Oven. Oven tray. Acrylic paints.
Paintbrushes. Green polymer clay (a large piece). Goldfish bowl. Water.

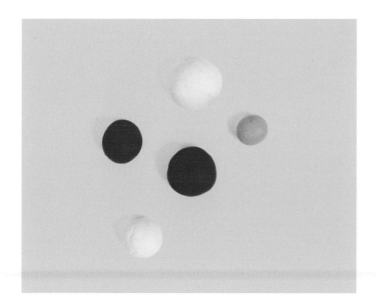

1. Roll pieces of polymer clay into balls roughly the size of a grape.

2. Flatten the balls into discs, either by hand, or using a rolling pin.

23

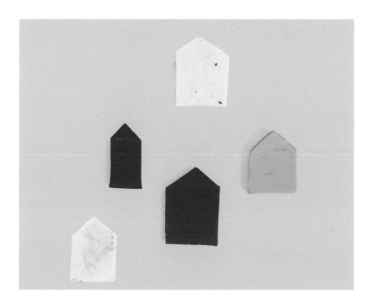

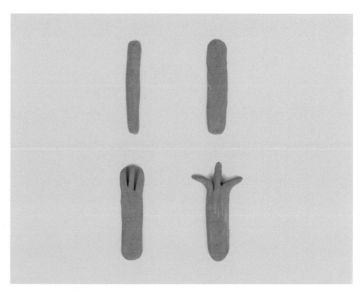

3. Cut the flat pieces into house shapes with the butter knife. Make as many of these flat houses as you want in your city.

4. Using more polymer clay, make flat tree and bush shapes too.

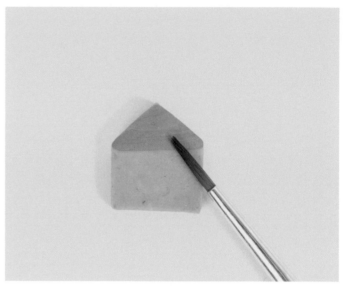

24 5. Set the clay shapes in the oven according to the packet instructions. Ask an adult to help.

6. Once cooled and hard, paint on details with acrylic paints.

7. Paint windows and doors onto the houses, and leaves onto the bushes and trees. Let the paint dry.

8. Shape a hill from a large piece of green polymer clay.

9. Check that your hill fits neatly into the bottom of your goldfish bowl.

10. Firmly press the houses and trees into the clay hill.

11. Carefully lower the city into the bowl, and press it down onto the glass so that it grips and sticks.

12. Gently and slowly pour water into the goldfish bowl so your city is submerged.

26

costume design

What do your clothes say about you?

Can clothes talk?

Messages sent by masks and costumes

1

2

A mask or a costume is a way of saying something about the person wearing it. We wear costumes that say something about us all the time. Think of a chef's hat and uniform. It tells everyone "I know how to cook!"

We make judgments about people based on what they wear. So we might think a person in a smart suit is serious, or a person wearing a doctor's white coat and glasses is clever. Actors wear costumes or masks to help show the character they play.

27

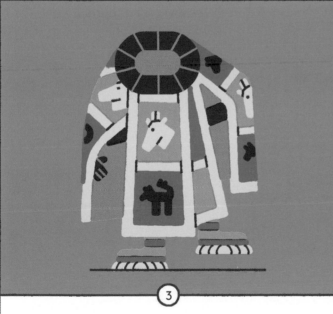

3

4

People around the world wear special outfits on religious occasions. A costume might be used to act out a religious story, or to help the person wearing it feel like they are "becoming" a different person or spirit.

Many artists have been interested by how costumes and masks let us feel like we are different people, or in a different imaginary place. On the next page you will see Damien Poulain's masks. They are meant to transport the wearer to a fantastical world of candy!

<u>Damien Poulain</u> makes amazing masks out of candy. Whoever puts them on becomes a traveler from Planet Sweet. Are you ready to join them?

He named his series:
"Masks & Sweets"

28

"The masks are designed to lead you to a different reality."

Dress up as your favorite object.

Who are you today?

How do you feel when you wear a costume?

Design an outfit you could wear for sport or a hobby.

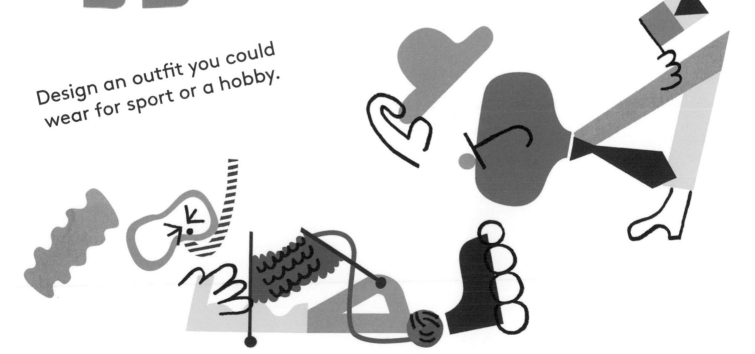

Fantastical pasta masks

Who would you rather be?
A six-eyed monster or a cyclops?

→ YOU WILL NEED:
Cardboard. Paints. Paintbrush. Dried pasta shapes. Scissors.
Pencil. Eraser. School glue. Tape.

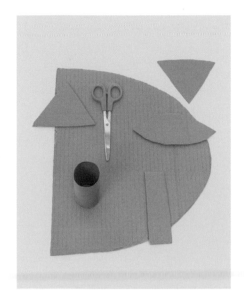

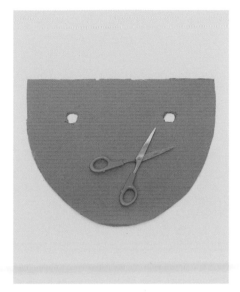

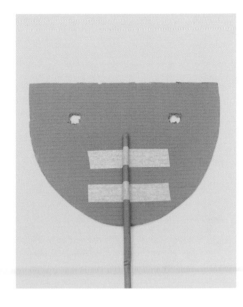

1. Draw the shape of your mask on pieces of cardboard, and cut them out.

2. The holes are easier to cut out if you push a pencil through the mask into an eraser first.

3. Tape a pencil or a chopstick to the back of your mask to make a handle.

31

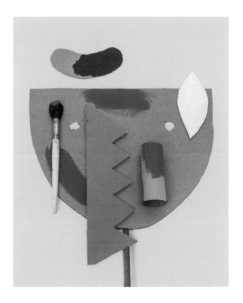

4. Paint the pasta pieces different colors, and leave them to dry.

5. Paint the cardboard pieces in bright colors. When they are dry, try out designs with the pasta and cardboard.

6. Once you're happy with your design, glue the all pieces in place. Now you can become a monster.

Superpower cape

Look into the future!

You have superpowers and you need a cape.

A large piece of plain fabric. Felt in different colors.
Fabric glue. A long piece of ribbon.

1. Find a piece of material like an old sheet, and cut it into a rectangle.

2. Think of a design that shows your superpower. Create that design by cutting shapes from colored felt.

33

3. Leaving the top 10cm of your cape plain, glue the felt design onto your cape following the instructions on the bottle.

4. Turn the cape over and lay the ribbon 5cm from the cape's top edge. Fold the edge down over the ribbon and glue it, making a kind of tube the ribbon is trapped inside. Let it dry.

34

illustrate

A surprise for your eyes!

Why do some pictures stick?

Illustration that surprises

1

Have you ever heard the saying "a picture is worth a thousand words?" You could say this about an illustration. Illustration is a way to show and tell people something quickly. Like this picture. You can instantly see what has happened without being told.

2

But your illustration won't tell anyone anything if no one is paying attention. We are bombarded with images all the time, from advertments, to packaging, to pictures in the news. It's hard for one image to catch your attention, to really make you look and remember.

3

SURPRISE! That's a way to get peoples' attention. By making a picture that is in some way surprising or unexpected, you can make people notice and remember. Visual humor can do this, for example by combining opposites or lookalike objects, like a wizard wearing a traffic cone instead of a hat.

4

Another way to make your picture surprising is to show something familiar in a new way. On the next page, Sarah Illenberger has illustrated the ingredients for chilli con carne. Instead of simply photographing the ingredients (boring), she has made 3D paper models (new).

Sarah Illenberger works with everyday objects and materials to create visual surprises that stick. Here she illustrated a column describing the cooking process of a very complex recipe.

The recipe is for:
"Chilli Con Carne"

"I think of my paper sculptures as three-dimensional illustration."

How can a familiar object look new?

Which animals do your friends and family look like?

Opposites
+
lookalikes

What object do you look like most?

Think of opposites, like a bald bear and a hairy egg.

37

Tutti frutti

Hurry up and take the picture before someone eats your fruit!

→ YOU WILL NEED:
Fruit. Pencil. Plain paper. Colored paints.
Paintbrush. Scissors. Camera.

1. Choose a selection of fruit as your starting point.

2. Think about what the fruits remind you of. What else could they represent? Draw out some ideas.

3. When you have a good idea, paint some paper with patterns and bright colors to use in your picture.

39

4. We are making a space scene, so we have drawn planets and rays of light. Draw and cut out shapes you need.

5. Arrange your fruit with the cut-out paper pieces to give it a new identity. Add in hand-drawn details too.

6. Photograph your artwork from above. If you feel ambitious you could add some characters to the final scene.

Sporty stones

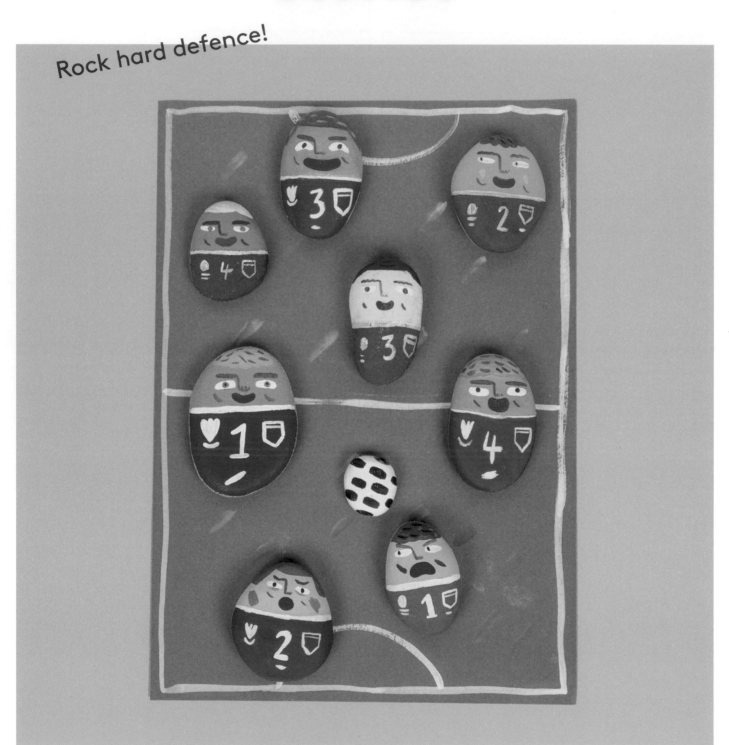

Rock hard defence!

A speedy sports team stands
as still as stone statues.

→ YOU WILL NEED:
Smooth pebbles. Pencil. Paintbrush. Acrylic paints.
Sheet of cardboard. Poster paints.

1. Who are your favorite sports team? Collect smooth pebbles for each team member. Don't forget a ball!

2. Using acrylic paints, paint the shirt color onto the bottom half of each stone, and the face color on top.

3. When dry, draw details such as the shirt number and face onto each stone in pencil.

41

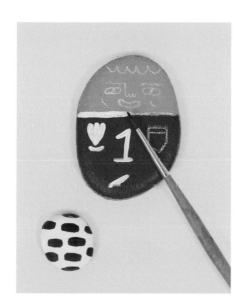

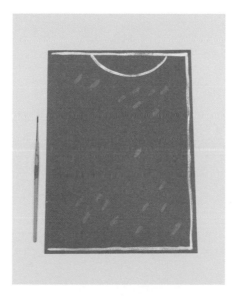

4. Paint on the details again using acrylic paint, and leave to dry. Don't forget the ball.

5. Make a field by painting a piece of cardboard with poster paint. Be sure to add all the markings and goals.

6. Arrange the team on the field. You can do the same for the the opposing team.

42

paper craft

Symmetries and silhouettes

Can old crafts still inspire?

Playing with paper

1

Paper is a cheap and widely available material. From ancient Chinese paper cuttings to Mexican *papel picado*, folk artists around the world have made use of the beautiful shapes and symmetry that paper cutting and crafting can create.

2

In Europe in the 18th century, having your portrait painted was a luxury only the rich could afford. But a silhouette — a soild shadow outline of your head in profile — cut out of black paper was a popular and affordable alternative.

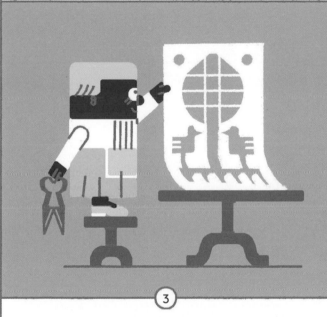

3

Polish peasants in the 19th century decorated their homes with paper cuttings made using large sheep-shearing scissors. The paper cuttings showed seasonal and religious images, such as cockerels at Easter, as well as symmetrical, geometric designs.

4

On the next page you can see paper cuttings by Henning Wagenbreth, who has been inspired by this traditional art form. He has used paper cutting to show new, contemporary images full of strange and surprising creatures and machines.

<u>Henning Wagenbreth</u> creates his own strange world of paper cuttings filled with human-like buildings, weird machines and two-headed creatures.

He named his series:
"!WOW! Symmetrical Papercuts'"

44

"The biggest joy comes the moment when I unfold the cut paper and see something unexpected."

Sketch symmetrical patterns.

Shine a light on objects and draw the shadows they make.

Draw outlines of things you can see around you.

Mirrors + shadows

Draw a symmetrical face on gridded paper.

45

Paper people

Our paper people take Henning Wagenbreth's
paper cuttings as inspiration.

→ YOU WILL NEED:
Some large pieces of colored paper in contrasting colors.
Scissors. Pencil. Glue stick.

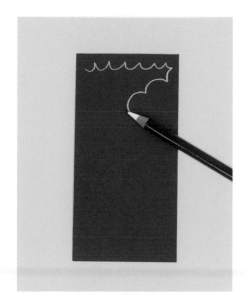

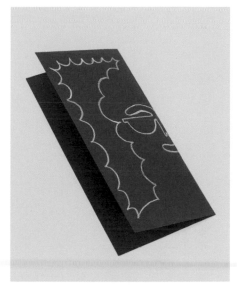

1. Sketch some paper people. Think about the two matching halves of a face.

2. Fold a big piece of colored paper in half lengthways. Draw half of your design. The fold is the center line.

3. To create a frame shape, draw a line that attaches to both the top and bottom of the face shape.

4. Cut around your design, through both halves of the folded card. Be careful not to cut through the design itself.

5. Open it to reveal your symmetrical art. Try different contrasting paper underneath.

6. Glue pieces of the colored paper to the back of your cut-out. Flip it over and see your finished face.

Restless shapes

48

A mobile is a type of moving sculpture.
Create paper shapes that shift and swing.

→ YOU WILL NEED:
Colored paper. Paints. Paintbrush. Scissors.
Pencil. String. Hole punch. Ribbon. A thin stick about 12 in. long.

1. Look around your town. Draw some simple shapes that show what you see.

2. Paint patterns onto sheets of colored paper.

3. Copy the shapes you saw in your town on the colored paper. Cut them out, and punch a hole in each piece.

49

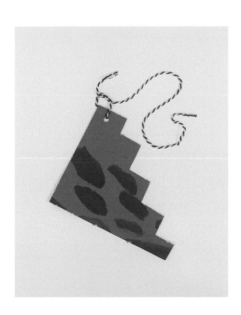

4. Cut several pieces of string 8-12 in. long. Tie a paper shape in the middle and at the end of each piece of string.

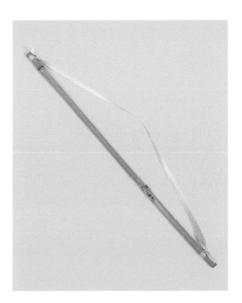

5. Cut a piece of ribbon or string about one and a half times as long as your stick. Tie the ribbon on at each end.

6. Tie the strings with the paper pieces around the stick. Spread them evenly. Hang your mobile using the ribbon.

Do the robot

Street dancing shadow bots

Play music and make them dance!

→ YOU WILL NEED:
Pencil, Paper, Eraser, Thin black card, Scissors, Metal fasteners,
Thin sticks or skewers, Sticky tape, White sheet, Lamp.

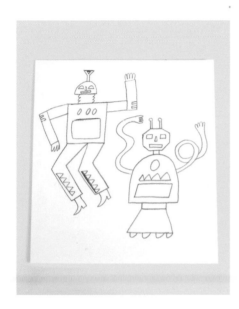

1. Robots have taken over the world. They are battling it out in a dance-off. Sketch what your robot looks like.

2. Draw the head and body, arms and legs as separate pieces onto black card. Leave a half inch tab on each limb for the hinge. Cut them out.

3. Cut out details within the shapes by poking a pencil into a eraser through the card, then snipping with scissors. Don't forget eyes.

51

4. Attach the limbs with metal fasteners. Hold the pieces together and pierce holes with a pencil. Insert the fastener and press open its ends.

5. Tape bamboo skewers to the back of the puppet, one on each moveable part.

6. Make a theatre by hanging a sheet with a lamp behind. Hold your puppets between the sheet and the lamp.

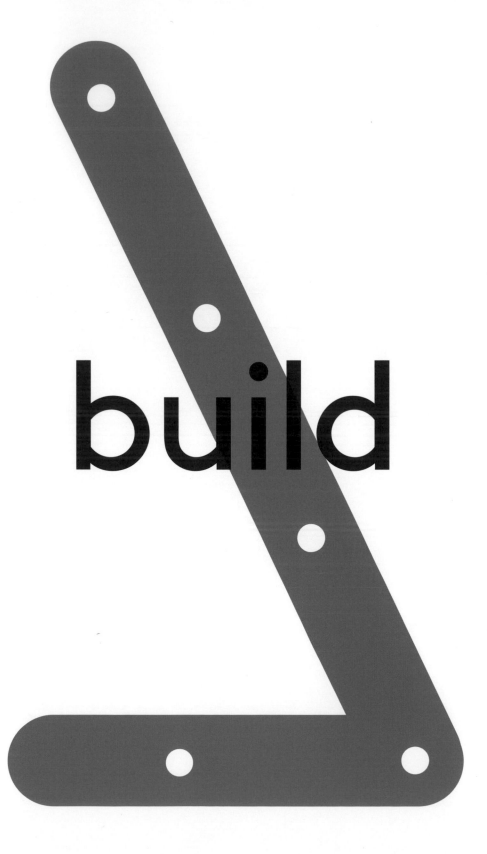

build

BUILD

Big art that questions how we live

Can buildings change lives?

Big art about big ideas

1

Throughout the last hundred years, many artists and architects have been interested in the question of what a perfect world, called a "utopia," would be like. What would it look like? How would people live? What would the buildings be like?

2

The way a room or house is designed can change how we feel, or even behave. A dark, cramped room can make you unhappy. In a group of houses with a shared garden, you might talk to your neighbors more.

53

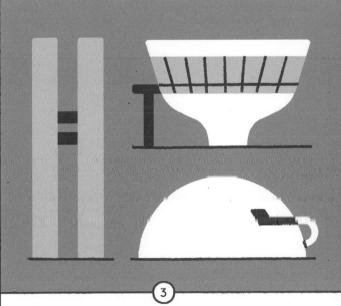

3

In the 1960s, architects tried to design buildings that would make life better for the residents. Artists like the Haus-Rucker-Co group created "installations" — big 3D artworks that you can go inside — so people could experience being in a mini-utopia.

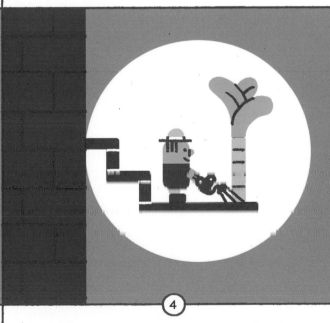

4

Haus-Rucker-Co were an architectural collective who built several inflatable installations in the 1960s and 70s. Their playful creations encouraged the public to think about space and how we interact with it. See one of their works, "Oasis No.7'"on the next page.

<u>Haus-Rucker-Co</u> designed this temporary, inflatable room. It emerges from an existing building, creating a space for relaxation and play.

Who wouldn't like to hang out at "Oasis No. 7?"

54

"Oasis No. 7 shows the dream of city dwellers for nature."

Draw a house full of inventions that would make your life better.

What's the best thing that could happen to your city?

Dreams + nightmares

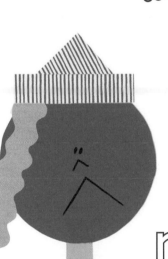

55

What's the worst thing that could happen to your city?

What inventions would make your life worse?

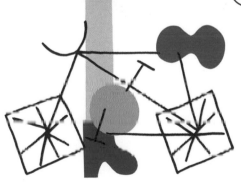

Sci-fi city

King for a day!

What will the future look like if you
are the one in charge?

→ YOU WILL NEED:
Three large pieces of card. Pencil.
Scissors. Paper. Paints. Paintbrush.

1. Sketch designs for the houses and buildings in your amazing sci-fi city.

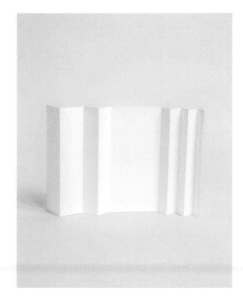

2. Fold three bits of cardboard into concertinas. The distance between the folds can vary.

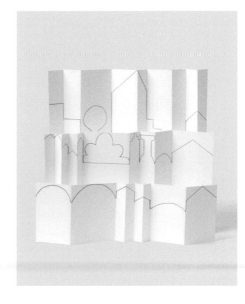

57

3. Draw a row of houses on each folded card. Make the back row tall, and the front row short.

4. Cut along the roofs of each of the three pieces of card.

5. Paint the houses in bright colors and patterns, and leave to dry.

6. Cut out window shapes. Find a place to display your city and stand the sections in height order.

Print your street

58

Take a walk down your street.
Are you inspired by what you see?

→ YOU WILL NEED:
Pencil and paper. Foam board. Ballpoint pen. Acrylic paint. Paintbrush.
Roller or rolling pin. Scissors. Large piece of paper. Glue stick.

1. Sketch some houses on your street. Place a sketch on top of a piece of foam board of the same size.

2. Use a ball point pen to draw over your drawing, pressing firmly to leave an indentation in the foam.

3. Use acrylic paints to fill in your design on the foam board. Then use the end of a paintbrush to scrape details into the paint.

59

4. Place a piece of plain paper over your painting. Use a small roller or rolling pin to press the paper firmly.

5. Peel off your print and cut it out carefully with scissors.

6. Use this method to print the rest of the buildings and trees in your street. Stick them into one large design.

A perfect space

60

If you could build your dream room,
what would it look like?

→ YOU WILL NEED:
Pencil and paper. Several pieces of thin plain card.
Poster paints. Paintbrush.

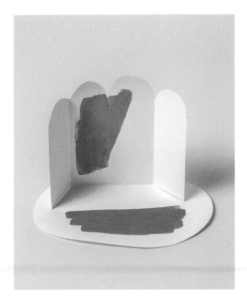

1. What would your perfect room look like? We're making a dinosaur room.

2. Fold a piece of thin card into three to make the sides of your room. Cut a large circle from another piece for the floor.

3. Cut the top into shapes too if you like. Paint the walls and floor using poster paint.

61

4. To make the furniture and accessories, draw them onto thin card, leaving 1 in. tabs to fold and stand them with.

5. Paint the pieces with poster paint, and cut them out when dry. Fold the tabs backwards so they stand.

6. Try the pieces in different positions until it looks perfect. Then glue the tabs to the floor of your perfect room.

62

work together

Many hands make light work

Why make art together?

How artists collaborate to create exciting art

(1)

Usually, artworks are made by only one artist, as most artists like to have complete control over what they are creating. But sometimes there are good reasons to work in teams.

(2)

Some really big art requires a lot of people to work together. The "Names" project involved 94,000 people, who worked together to make a giant 54 ton quilt commemorating people who had died from AIDS.

(3)

Sometimes, artists who share particular interests or ways of making art work together as a collective. In this way, the final piece contains several people's ideas and skills. Haus-Rucker-Co, from the previous chapter, is an example of a collective.

(4)

Working together can also be very exciting, because it can produce unpredictable results. Yayoi Kusama lets the audience help create her work. The result is the beautiful interactive installation you can see on the next page.

Yayoi Kusama is obsessed with dots. Her artwork is often covered in them! Here the audience were given dot stickers to place wherever they liked, covering an entirely white room.

This collaborative artwork is called:
"The Obliteration Room"

"Polka-dots can't stay alone ...
Polka-dots are a way to infinity."

How does it feel to work in a team?

Challenge a friend to turn a squiggle into a picture.

Team play

Think of an idea for an artwork that would need a thousand artists.

Draw a busy market scene with a friend.

65

Head
body legs

Go on, spin some limbs!

Mix the body with your buddies.

→ YOU WILL NEED:
Nine square cardboard boxes. Poster paints. Paintbrushes.

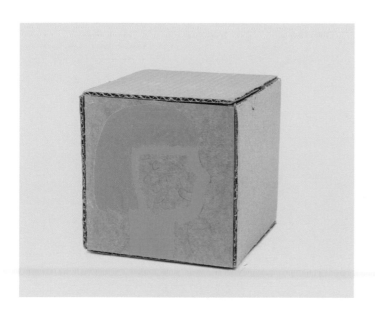

1. You will need three people, and three cardboard boxes each. Everybody paints a head on their first box, a body on their second box, and a pair of legs on their third box.

2. Once dry, swap boxes with someone else. Paint another set of head, body and legs on the blank sides of your new boxes.

3. Swap boxes with the third person, and paint a new set of head, body, and legs on the blank sides, so each person has painted something on every box.

4. When the paint is dry, stack the boxes on top of each other in threes to make a character. See how many different characters you can make by spinning the boxes.

Monster mash

Do the monster mâché

→ YOU WILL NEED:
Pencil. Paper. Newspaper. Foil. Acrylic paints. Paintbrush.
Scissors. School glue. Water. A shallow tray. Tape.

1. You will need a party of people. Each sketch a monster to make. Give each monster a different dance move.

2. Screw up pieces of newspaper into balls. This will be the stuffing of your monsters.

69

3. Wrap the paper in foil, and pinch the top to make a head shape.

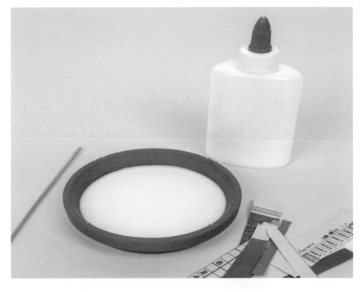

4. Make a mix of equal parts water and school glue, and pour it into a shallow tray. Tear newspaper into strips, and dip the strips in the tray of glue mix, so they get soaked.

70   5. Lay the glue-soaked strips onto the foil body, and smooth them down with your fingers.

6. Cover the body with overlapping papier mâché pieces. Do a few layers using this technique, making sure that you let the glue dry fully between layers.

7. Leave the body to dry out completely and go hard. This can take a couple of days.

8. Once dried and hard, paint the body in your favorite monster color.

9. Draw the limbs on some cardboard. Make sure the feet are nice and sturdy. Cut the limbs out.

10. Paint the limbs bright colors, adding pattern and texture.

11. Stick the legs and feet together with glue. If necessary, use sticky tape to make them sturdy.

12. When the body is dry, glue on the legs, arms and tail. Put everybody's monsters together on the dance floor!

shoot

Photography that shows your
inside on the outside

A photo of your personality?

How portraiture can show more than what we look like.

(1)

People have taken portraits — pictures of people — since photography was invented. In the early days having your picture taken was a serious business, so people didn't smile. Taking a photo took 20 minutes! Now it's easy to take a picture at any time, anywhere.

(2)

Selfies are a massively popular kind of photographic portraiture. With selfies we try to be in control of how other people see us. When we share pictures of ourselves having fun with friends we might want to appear popular or simply share a happy moment.

73

(3)

When a photographer takes a portrait, they can carefully plan the picture so that it says a lot about who that person is. Through the choice of clothes, location and props, they can communicate a lot of information about someone's personality.

(4)

On the next page, Ilona Szwarc's portrait of a young Rodeo Girl seems like a simple image.
But look closely and you can see that the country location, her hat, her expression and her belt are giving you clues about her personality and her hobby.

<u>Ilona Szwarc</u> spent a summer in Texas shooting portraits of girls who compete in the macho world of rodeo riding. The girls embrace the traditionally male image of the cowboy — hard work and discipline.

Hi "Rodeo Girls!"

"This series is about the different ways
of being a girl in the United States."

What things in your bedroom reveal your hobbies?

Take a portrait of a pet showing off its personality.

What is your favorite self-portrait and why?

Show yourself

75

Take photos of your three most prized posessions.

Portrait with props

Snappy snaps!

Have you got an animal hiding inside?

→ YOU WILL NEED:
Paper. Pencil. Large pieces of cardboard. Poster paints. Paintbrushes.
Scissors. Camera. Stepladder or chair. A friend.

1. Sketch which animal your personality is most like. We've chosen a shark, so have made plant and fish props.

2. Draw outlines for your prop pieces on cardboard.

3. Cut out and paint the prop pieces using poster paints. Leave them to dry.

4. Paint details on the pieces.

5. Find a large, flat area of ground that can be the backdrop to your photo. Lay your props out in a scene.

6. Try out different positions with the props and have someone stand on a chair to photograph you from above.

Drawing on portraits

78

A blank canvas is overrated.
Start with a photo instead

→ YOU WILL NEED:
Photos printed out, or cut from magazines. Pencil. Paper.
Scissors. Acrylic paints. Paintbrush.

1. Find some pictures of your family and friends and print them out. Make sure you ask before using original photographs! Alternatively use pictures from magazines.

2. How can you show someone's personality? You could change their clothes, make up, where they are, or add their favorite things. Sketch your ideas on a separate piece of paper.

79

3. First decide on the background and use acrylic paint to add your ideas directly to the photograph.

4. Add details on top. You can do this for your whole family — make an album!

Cover Ola Niepsuj, *think and make like an artist,* 2016 **9** Jay Daniel Wright, *What is a painting?,* 2016 **10** Cornelia Baltes, *Dingbats,* 2013, Acrylic on canvas and wood, 130 x 120 cm, Limoncello Gallery London **11** Ola Niepsuj, *Play with paint,* 2016 **17** Jay Daniel Wright, *Why make sculptures?,* 2016 **18** James Drive, Hot with the chance of a late storm, 2006, polystyrene with a urethane coat, 6 x 6 x 1 m, private collection, photograph © Derek Henderson **19** Ola Niepsuj, *Love or Hate,* 2016 **27** Jay Daniel Wright, *Can clothes talk?,* 2016 **28** Damien Poulain, *Masks and sweets,* 2011, mixed media, private collection, photograph © Thomas Adank **29** Ola Niepsuj, *Who are you today?,* 2016 **35** Jay Daniel Wright, *Why do some pictures stick?,* 2016 **36** Sarah Ilenberger, *Chili con carne,* 2009, paper, private collection, photograph © Ragnar Schmuck **37** Ola Niepsuj, *Opposites + Lookalikes,* 2016 **43** Jay Daniel Wright, *Can traditional crafts inspire?,* 2016 **44** Henning Wagenbreth, *!WOW! Symmetrical Papercuts Poster,* 2014, silkscreen print, 70 x 100 cm, private collection **45** Ola Niepsuj, *Mirrors + shadows,* 2016 **53** Jay Daniel Wright *Can buildings change lives?,* 2016 **54** Haus-Rucker-Co, (Laurids Ortner, Manfred Ortner, Klaus Pinter and Günter Zamp Kelp) *Oasis No. 7,* documenta 5, Kassel, 1972, plastic and metal, 8 x 8 m, photograph © documenta Archiv **55** Ola Niepsuj, Dreams + nightmares, 2016 **63** Jay Daniel Wright, *Why make art together?,* 2016 **63** Jay Daniel Wright, *Why make art together?,* 2016 **64** Yayoi Kusama, *The Obliteration Room,* 2002 to present, furniture, white paint, dot stickers. Collaboration between Yayoi Kusama and Queensland Art Gallery. Commissioned Queensland Art Gallery, Australia. Gift of the artist through the Queensland Art Gallery Foundation 2012 Collection: Queensland Art Gallery, Brisbane, photograph: Mark Sherwood, QAGOMA © Yayoi Kusama **65** Ola Niepsuj, *Team play,* 2016 **66** Jay Daniel Wright, *A photo of your personality?,* 2016 **67** Ilona Szwarc, *Rodeo Girls,* 2012, private collection **68** Ola Niepsuj, *Show yourself,* 2016